My Magical Pony

Falling Leaves

The **My Magical Pony** series:

Other series by Jenny Oldfield:

My Magical Pony

Falling Leaves

By Jenny Oldfield

Illustrated by Gillian Martin

Hodder
Children's
Books

A division of Hachette Children's Books

Text copyright © 2006 Jenny Oldfield
Illustrations copyright © 2006 Gillian Martin

First published in Great Britain in 2006
by Hodder Children's Books

The rights of Jenny Oldfield and Gillian Martin to be identified as the
Author and Illustrator of the Work respectively have been asserted by them in
accordance with the Copyright, Designs and Patents Act 1988.

1

A Catalogue record for this book is available from the British Library

ISBN-10: 0 340 91843 8
ISBN-13: 9780340918432

Printed and bound in Great Britain by
Bookmarque Ltd, Croydon, Surrey

The paper and board used in this paperback by Hodder Children's Books are
natural recyclable products made from wood grown in sustainable forests. The
manufacturing processes conform to the environmental
regulations of the country of origin.

Hodder Children's Books
a division of Hachette Children's Books
338 Euston Road, London NW1 3BH

Hodder Children's Books Australia
Hachette Children's Books
Level 17/207 Kent Street
Sydney, NSW 2000

Chapter One

Krista leaned on the fence watching Duchess and her foal, Frankie. The chestnut mare nudged the foal away from a muddy patch by the gate, but naughty Frankie took it into his head to have a good roll in the mud. Down he went on to his knees, rolling on his back and covering himself in muck from head to toe.

Krista laughed. OK, so she would be the one who would have to take Frankie in later and brush him clean, but she couldn't help smiling at the way he'd disobeyed his mum and had fun.

My Magical Pony

Duchess and Frankie trotted towards her.
She met them at the gate, first making a fuss of
the mother then stroking little Frankie's face.

"You're filthy!" she told him. "You've only
been at Hartfell for a few days, and already
you're getting way too cheeky!"

Falling Leaves

Frankie nudged her hand with his nose. *More strokes, please!*

"See!" Krista laughed.

She'd been thrilled when Jo Weston, the owner of Hartfell stables, had bought the mare and foal at a local horse sale.

"The mother is a Connemara cross," Jo had told Krista as they'd unloaded the new arrivals from the trailer. "And look at the foal. How sweet is he?"

A gawky chestnut foal had appeared at the top of the ramp. He had a big head and long legs, with a white star on his forehead and four gorgeous white socks.

Krista had adored Frankie right from the start.

My Magical Pony

Now, as she stood petting him before she
went to begin a day's work at the yard, she
chanted an old rhyme Jo had taught her.

"One white sock, send him right away
Two white socks, have him but a day
Three white socks, give him to a friend
Four white socks, keep him to the end!

"You have four white socks, so you're going
to stay here for ever," Krista murmured to
Frankie.

The foal stretched his neck and took a
nibble at the zip on her pocket.

"Hey!" she protested, pulling free and
stooping to pick up her bike. "Anyway, I've
got to go."

Frankie raised his head and gave a shrill

whinny. He trotted alongside the fence as Krista pedalled on up the lane.

"I'll see you later, you little monkey!" Laughing and looking forward to the day ahead, Krista cycled towards the stables.

"That's odd!" Krista looked round the deserted yard. To one side the barn was stacked with bales of hay. A row of empty stables linked the barn to the tack room. Krista tried the tack room door and found that it was locked.

"Where's Jo?" she said to herself, peering into each stable then turning to look at the house which stood on the far side of the yard. All the curtains were closed and there was no sign of life.

9

My Magical Pony

Checking her watch, Krista saw that it was eight o'clock – way past the time when Jo was normally up and about. And today, Saturday, was her busiest day.

Weird! Krista thought. *Well, I can't do anything if the tack room's locked,* she decided. *So I'd better go and wake Jo up.*

She was about to cross the yard and knock on Jo's door when she heard a car coming up the lane. Soon Jo's friend Rob Buckley arrived in his rusty old Land Rover.

"Hey, Krista!" Rob called. "Jo's sick. Did you know?"

Shaking her head, Krista hurried across. "What's wrong with her?"

Rob shrugged. "I don't know exactly. I just

Falling Leaves

got a call. She said she felt so lousy she couldn't even get out of bed. I said I'd drop in and see if I could help."

Waiting for Rob to use his key to unlock Jo's front door, Krista went into the house with him.

"Hi, cats!" Rob said, as Holly and Lucy, Jo's two black cats, rushed across the hallway to greet them.

Krista bent to stroke them and went to check in the kitchen to see that they had milk to drink. Meanwhile Rob went upstairs.

He quickly came down to use the phone. "Jo's pretty bad," he reported. "She says she aches all over and hasn't got the energy to get up. I'm going to call the doctor."

"Wow!" Krista knew this was serious. Jo was the sort who never got sick. So while Rob rung the surgery, she went upstairs to Jo's room.

"Hi," Krista said, poking her head around the door.

"Oh Krista, hi," Jo's voice was weak. She lay flat on her back, unable to sit up. "Sorry about this," she sighed. "But it looks like I'll have to cancel today's lessons. Do you think you could make a few phone calls for me?"

"Sure." Krista found out which pupils were due to have lessons and promised to

phone them. "Is Rob sticking around?"

Jo nodded. "He says he'll stay for the whole day and supervise the treks. So at least people will still be able to ride out."

"Cool. I'll start bringing the ponies in." Krista was glad to spring into action. Sickrooms weren't her thing – she never knew what to say. Soon she was downstairs and out of the house, heading for the tack room with the key. *Head collars and lead ropes. First things first!*

Krista knew they would need six ponies for today's riders. She chose Shandy and Drifter, Comanche of course, Woody for Holly Owen, Misty for Alice and finally Kiki for herself. It took her almost half an hour to bring them all in.

13

My Magical Pony

"I thought Nathan could ride Drifter," she told Rob, who by this time had begun to groom the ponies. "And Comanche and Shandy will be good for the two new kids."

"Good thinking," Rob replied. Dust and loose hair flew from Shandy's dark brown coat as he brushed hard. "Can you bring Scottie for me? I'd better lead the trek and keep an eye on things."

Nodding, Krista went back for the big chestnut gelding, an ex-racehorse who Jo had bought from a flat-race trainer. He was in a field with Jo's own horse, Apollo.

"Sorry, 'Pollo, I didn't come for you," Krista told the big grey thoroughbred, who stuck his nose in her face. "Jo's not feeling too good.

14

Falling Leaves

She won't be riding today."

Instead she led Scottie out through the gate, passing close to Duchess and young Frankie's field. The two chestnuts were excited and trotted along on the other side of the fence.

15

My Magical Pony

"Look at Frankie!" Krista said to Scottie as she led him along the lane. "He's covered in mud. Isn't he a disgrace!"

Scottie ignored his admirers, stepping out with his head held high, his sleek neck arched.

Krista led him into the yard and tied him next to Shandy. "I have to make a few phone calls," she told Rob. "Then I'll help you tack up."

From the tack room she rang the numbers Jo had given her then dashed back outside. People were already arriving and cars were dropping off young riders for the morning trek.

"Hi, Alice. Hi, Nathan!" Krista greeted her friends with the news that Jo was sick, and the two early birds gladly lent Rob a hand with the grooming.

Falling Leaves

Then the doctor showed up and Rob took him into the house. He stayed for ten minutes then came out shaking his head.

"I can't put my finger on anything in particular," the doctor was telling Rob as the two men stood in the yard. "Her blood pressure's normal. She's been telling me about a bad headache and some vomiting during the night."

"It's not like her," Rob said. "I've never known Jo be ill. And I've been friends with her for over ten years."

"I know, I've looked at her notes and there's nothing on them. Her medical history is one big empty space. Anyway, I've told her to drink plenty of fluids and take it easy,"

the doctor went on, "and to call me again if she needs to."

Rob nodded and thanked him. "So you think she'll soon be back on her feet?"

The doctor shrugged. "Let's hope so."

From a few metres away, Krista nodded. *Yeah, let's hope so!* she thought. *I miss Jo already. And so do the ponies — especially Apollo!*

Chapter Two

The cool thing about riding was that when you were out on the trail, looking down at Whitton Bay and the white waves crashing against the shore, you forgot all your worries.

It's like stepping into a new world! Krista thought. She rode at the back of the group of riders making their way down to the beach. *Every time I sit in the saddle and hold the reins, I feel an adventure coming on!*

Today it was the excitement of riding with Rob, who took a new route down the cliff instead of the well-worn trail.

He led his six riders down steep, rocky slopes, between boulders on a zigzag course to the bottom, where the ponies stood at last on the flat sand.

"Wow, that was cool!" Nathan yelled, reining Drifter back.

"Let's go paddling!" cried Krista. Soon the ponies were knee-deep in the swirling waves, splashing spray and making their riders shriek.

"Wicked!" Alice cried. Misty plunged deeper into the sea, setting a pace which the others followed.

"I'm soaking wet!" Holly shouted as Woody passed Misty.

Krista laughed, and set off at top speed, kicking up white spray.

20

Falling Leaves

Nathan was laughing his head off. "Is horse riding classed as an extreme sport?" he asked.

Rob grinned back at him. "It is now."

"Shouldn't you be in bed?" Rob asked Jo later that day.

My Magical Pony

He'd led the morning ride, then in the afternoon he'd taken out a second group while Krista had stayed behind to school Duchess in the open arena. When he got back, he found Jo up and dressed, watching her new mare at work.

"I feel better," Jo told him. "Take a look at Duchess. She has nice paces. Her transition from trot to canter is really smooth."

"Yes, but you should be taking it easy," Rob insisted. He'd said goodbye to a second bunch of happy riders and returned the ponies to their fields. Now he'd joined Jo to watch Krista and Duchess in the arena.

Krista concentrated on working the lunge line. She sent the chestnut mare in a

22

clockwise circle, then reined her in and sent her anti-clockwise. Duchess flicked her ears and swished her tail, paying attention and working hard.

"I stayed in bed all morning and then I got bored," Jo told Rob. "You know me – I can't stay away from my babies!"

"But you look awful," Rob insisted.

"Thanks!" Attempting to laugh it off, Jo asked Krista to walk Duchess in a straight line towards her. "Yep, she's a nice little pony," she confirmed. "I thought so the moment I set eyes on her."

"I brushed Frankie," Krista said, gathering in the lunge line and getting ready to take Duchess back to her field. "But the moment I put him back in the field, he rolled in the mud again!"

23

Jo smiled and nodded.

"Rob's right – you look really bad," Krista told her. Jo was pale, and her hand shook as she reached out to stroke Duchess's neck.

"I'll be fine. Stop fussing, both of you."

Krista turned to Rob, who shrugged and said, "You heard the lady!"

So Krista nodded and led Duchess off. She put the mare in her field, did the last jobs of the day then went to find Jo in the tack room.

Jo sat on a bench, stooped forward, with her head hanging as if she was exhausted. But she looked up when she heard Krista's footsteps.

"I'll be off then," Krista told her, hovering uncertainly by the door. Somehow she was

24

Falling Leaves

reluctant to leave.

Jo took a deep breath then nodded.

"See you tomorrow," Krista said.

Jo made what seemed like a big effort to smile. Her face was white, and there were dark circles under her normally lively eyes. "Yes, Krista, see you tomorrow," she replied.

Chapter Three

Next day was Sunday and Krista was up almost before it was light.

"Bring us a cup of tea, love!" her mum called from the bedroom as Krista crept by.

"Sorry, no time!" Krista popped her head around the door. "I have to be at Hartfell before seven."

"Tea!" her dad wailed, his head peeking out from under the duvet, one eye open, the other shut.

Krista's mum struck a deal. "If you make us a cuppa, your dad will drive you to the stables."

Falling Leaves

"OK!" Krista quickly agreed, trotting downstairs and leaving her dad wondering how the deal had come about without him even opening his mouth.

He stumbled downstairs just as the kettle was boiling. "How come you have to be early?" he asked Krista.

"Jo's been poorly. I want to make sure she doesn't do too much work."

Her dad rubbed his chin. "Hmm, I need a shave. So what's up with Jo?"

"Don't know. The doctor wasn't sure. He told her to take things easy."

"Which is like telling a dog not to bark or a cat not to miaow." Krista's dad knew the stable owner well. "Jo *never* eases up on her workload!"

My Magical Pony

Lifting the teabags from the mugs, Krista poured the milk. "Get dressed, Dad," she urged. "Come on, leave your tea to cool."

So he went upstairs while Krista dashed outside to put down a saucer of milk for her pet hedgehog, Spike.

"Sorry I can't stop to talk," she told the spiky little creature as he emerged from the hedge and snuffled his nose deep into the

saucer. "I've got to dash off. There's loads to do at Hartfell."

Slurp-slurp! Greedy Spike didn't care.

Falling Leaves

Back inside the house, she found her dad
still tousled and sleepy, but dressed and ready
to drive her to the stables. Soon they were
in the car and driving through the chilly
country lanes.

"It's definitely autumn," Krista's dad
grumbled as they drove into a mist. "The
leaves are turning brown. Pretty soon it'll
be winter, and we haven't even had any
summer yet!"

Krista tutted. Grown-ups were always
going on about the weather. "Stop the car,"
she told him as they drove up the lane to
Hartfell. She made him get out of the car to
take a look at Frankie. "Isn't he cute?"

Krista's dad gave a fake shiver. "Brrr!"

But when he saw the little chestnut foal running towards them through the mist, he nodded and smiled. "That is one cute pony!" he agreed.

Frankie trotted up to the fence.

"Hi, Frankie!" Krista gave him a quick stroke then jumped back in the car. "Sorry, can't stop – lots to do!"

Her dad drove on into the empty yard. Once more, Jo's curtains were closed.

"Uh-oh, that means she's still poorly," Krista sighed, but then she was relieved to see Jo pull back her bedroom curtains and wave at them.

Krista's dad waited until Jo came out of the house. "Are you OK?" he checked.

Falling Leaves

"Yes, I've got a touch of flu, that's all," she insisted, zipping up her thick fleece jacket. "I'll be over it in a day or two."

"Meanwhile, you've got an army of kids to give you a hand!" Krista's dad grinned as two more parents dropped their kids off.

Soon the yard was buzzing with helpers. Janey Bellwood was helping to prepare the tack while Krista and Nathan went out to the fields with head collars to bring the ponies in.

"Sit!" Janey told Jo. "Take it easy."

Nathan walked Drifter into his stable and came for currycombs and brushes. "Wow, Jo, are you sure you should be up?" he asked, glancing at her pale face and hunched figure.

31

My Magical Pony

"I wish I had a pound for every time someone has said that to me in the last twenty-four hours!" Jo grumbled. She was glad when Rob Buckley showed up again and took charge. "I'm going to make myself a cup of coffee and a slice of toast," she sighed, walking unsteadily towards the house.

Today Krista rode Scottie out along the lanes and bridleways, staying at the back of the group of riders led by Rob on Apollo. She sat straight in the saddle, looking over walls and hedges, watching the wind blow the brown leaves from the trees.

After a while, her mind drifted, and she thought of all the winding routes she'd ridden across the moors, in spring, summer, autumn

and winter. She went through the ponies of
Hartfell one by one.

  Do I have a favourite? Krista wondered.
*They're all really different! Kiki is skittish and spooks
at the least little thing. But she's fast and willing.*

33

My Magical Pony

Shandy's chunky and gorgeous and her coat shines when you brush it. Oh, and Comanche — well, Comanche …! Running out of words, Krista rode happily on.

"OK, thanks everyone!" At the end of the day, Rob called the helpers together in the yard at Hartfell.

There was no sign of Jo, who had been forced to go back to bed.

"Thanks, Krista." Rob singled her out. "I don't know what we'd have done without you."

Krista ducked her head and blushed. "I'm out of here!" she muttered, making a hasty exit out of the yard and down the lane on to the cliff path.

34

Falling Leaves

She walked quickly, wanting to get home in time to spend a few minutes in the garden with Spike before it grew dark. To one side, the cliff fell sheer to the beach. To the other, it rose in a steep slope to the rocky horizon.

Krista hurried on, only slowing down when she approached the magic spot. "Hi, Shining Star!" she said under her breath, in case her magical pony was listening. She never liked to pass this place without thinking about him and wondering where he was.

"Hello, Krista!" came the reply.

Her eyes widened and she stopped dead. "Hey, I didn't expect you to be here!" she gasped, looking up at the sky.

"Would you like to talk?" the voice asked.

My Magical Pony

Krista tried to make out a bright cloud
amongst the grey ones floating high over
Whitton Bay. The silvery cloud would mean
that her magical pony was nearby. Yes,
there it was – a distant sparkling shape,
separating itself and drawing nearer. "But I
never called you!"

Falling Leaves

"I think perhaps you will need me," Star said, approaching the magic spot and showering Krista with his glittering dust.

"Will I?" For a moment Krista tried to work out what Shining Star meant. She looked up and saw him emerge from the bright cloud, his magical wings spread wide as he hovered above her.

And then Star landed beside her and folded his wings. He held his head high and his dark eyes searched her face. "Krista," he said gently, "I sense trouble ahead."

"Do you mean Jo?" she asked shakily. "Did you know she was ill?"

Shining Star shook his head and his beautiful white mane flew back in the breeze.

37

"I did not. But I look ahead and see there is trouble for the ponies at Hartfell."

"Don't say that!" she pleaded, stepping up close and resting a hand on his neck. Suddenly the wind seemed cold and the sea roared way below.

"Listen, Jo will be better soon. It's nothing – she's got flu."

Star turned his head towards her. "I am here when you need me," he promised.

"I know you are." Krista's magical pony had never let her down, and she knew he was wise and saw things she couldn't see.

"Call me," he told her, spreading his wings again and showering silver dust all around.

She nodded. Her heart was beating fast

Falling Leaves

as Star rose into the sky. *Trouble for the ponies!* she thought.

And as her magical pony beat his wings and rose high into the sky, the truth struck her.

Jo has got something worse than flu! she realised. *This is serious. And if she's ill for a long time there'll be no one to look after the ponies!*

As Shining Star flew away, trailing his silver mist high over the sea, Krista stood alone on the magic spot, afraid to face tomorrow and what was to come.

Chapter Four

"So?" Krista sat on the lawn with Spike. It was Friday evening, and in spite of Shining Star's warning almost a week earlier, nothing bad had happened.

The little hedgehog rooted amongst the dead leaves under the bench. He kicked with his back feet to clear a space then began to dig furiously with his front paws to find a worm.

"So maybe Star was wrong," Krista murmured. Every day after school she'd cycled out to Hartfell to help Jo with the

usual chores. The weather had turned cold and they'd been bringing the ponies in at night, which meant mucking out and laying clean straw. Though Jo had been quiet and pale, she seemed much better than she had last weekend.

Spike gave up digging and, wormless, waddled up to the saucer of milk which Krista had put down.

"But Star is *never* wrong!" Krista tutted.

Hedgehog heaven! Spike slurped and swallowed.

"Talking to yourself?" Krista's dad had finished raking dead leaves into a pile at the bottom of the garden. He breezed by, heading towards the house for supper.

41

"Nope. I'm talking to Spike," Krista pointed out. She waited until her dad had disappeared then went on quietly. "The thing is, I'm not sure that Jo is really better," she confided to her prickly friend. "For instance, I got to the stables earlier tonight and found little Frankie caught by his head collar in the branches of a thorn bush. He was trapped and panicking and whinnying like crazy."

Falling Leaves

Spike finished his drink and came to sniff at Krista's boot.

"Normally Jo would never have left his head collar on in the field, or she would have spotted what was happening and gone out there to rescue him. But today she was in the house taking headache pills. I had to race down the field to free him. Luckily, he hadn't done himself any damage."

Spike sniffed at the left boot then moved on to concentrate on the right.

"*And!*" Krista went on. "Yesterday Apollo was limping on his back leg and Jo hadn't even noticed!" Come to think of it, that was unbelievable. Normally Jo would have picked up on that as soon as it had happened.

Krista sighed and stooped to pick up the empty saucer. "Luckily it's Saturday tomorrow and I've got all next week off school for half-term."

"Krista, supper time!" her mum called from the house.

Krista crouched right down for one last word with Spike. "Watch this space!" she said hurriedly. "I'm keeping my fingers crossed that nothing bad is going to happen, but I'll let you know if it does!"

Next morning, early as usual, Krista cycled the cliff path towards Hartfell. It was a bright, sunny autumn day with no clouds in the sky.

But when she reached the yard, she was disappointed to find no sign of Jo, and though

44

the curtains were open in the house, the place was strangely quiet.

"Hi, Jo!" Krista called, propping her bike against the wall and zipping her jacket up to her chin. She saw the ponies standing at their stable doors, patiently waiting to be let out. "Hi, Kiki. Hi, Comanche." Krista went along the row, giving each one a pat.

Scottie lowered his head and snorted, obviously expecting to ride out with Krista.

"So where's Jo?" she asked Duchess, stabled at the end of the row with young Frankie. She noticed that the stable was badly soiled and that the foal had rolled and covered himself in muck. "Yuck!" she grimaced, running to the tack room for a barrow and a spade.

45

Krista pushed at the door. "Huh, it's stuck!" she muttered, glancing back at the house, half expecting to see Jo come out of the front door. She pushed again.

Once more, the door refused to budge.

"Weird!" Something heavy was in the way. Krista peered through the gap. She saw a large, humped shape in the semi-darkness. Then she recognised the red fleece jacket and saw that it was a body collapsed on the floor.

"Jo!" Stunned, Krista stopped pushing. Jo was lying in the tack room without moving – probably unconscious, maybe even ... "No!" Quick as a flash, Krista ran to the window and wrenched at the handle. The window was locked. She ran back to the door.

46

Falling Leaves

Inside the room, Jo groaned and tried to move.

She was alive! Krista gave a sigh of relief. "Jo, it's me, Krista! Can you roll away from the door and let me in?"

Slowly and clumsily, Jo moved a few centimetres across the floor. She groaned as if she was in pain.

My Magical Pony

Krista eased the door open and slid through the gap. She dropped to her hands and knees. "What's wrong?" she cried, taking Jo's hand, but unsure what to do next.

"Call an ambulance," Jo whispered, her eyes half shut. "I don't know what happened. I must have fainted."

Krista was all fingers and thumbs as she pressed the buttons on her mobile phone. "We need an ambulance," she told the emergency operator. "My friend's sick. I've found her collapsed on the floor!"

Groaning again as she breathed in, Jo nodded and closed her eyes, "Give them the details. Thanks, Krista!"

"Wake up, Jo!" Krista pleaded, trying to

48

give the emergency services the information they needed. "She's fainted again!" she told the woman. "Tell them to hurry! Yes, to Hartfell Stables. Yes, she's breathing, but she's unconscious. No, I don't know when it happened. I just found her when I got here!"

At last the woman promised to send an ambulance straight away and Krista came off the phone. She searched Jo's face for any sign of life. "Jo," she whispered. "Please wake up!"

Jo's eyes stayed closed. Krista bent low over her face to check her breathing. She waited for what seemed like an age until at last the ambulance siren sounded on the lane then in the yard.

My Magical Pony

Waah-waah! Waah-waah! The noise seemed to break through to Jo, whose eyelids flickered. She opened her eyes and spoke. "Look after the ponies for me," she murmured, her voice sounding thick and blurred.

Krista kept hold of Jo's hand as the paramedics rushed through the door.

Falling Leaves

"Don't worry, they'll be fine!"

A man and a woman came in and eased Krista to one side. "It's OK, we'll take over now," the woman said, quickly examining Jo's pulse while the man unrolled a stretcher.

"Krista, take care of my babies!" Jo pleaded as she was attached to a monitor, lifted on to the stretcher and carried away.

"I will, I promise!" Krista replied. It seemed as if the world had done a giant somersault and everything had landed upside down. And here she was, just a kid, giving a grown-up her word that the ponies at Hartfell would come to no harm.

"Better get a move on!" the ambulance woman warned, checking the monitor.

Smoothly and efficiently they slid the stretcher into the ambulance. The woman stayed in the back with Jo while the man ran to the front and turned on the engine and sirens.

Waah-waah! The ambulance pulled out of the yard and sped down the lane.

Krista stood and listened to the silence, staring up at the empty grey sky.

Chapter Five

"It's no good, we'll have to cancel everything," Rob decided as soon as he arrived.

Krista had told him about the ambulance and he was anxious to drive to the hospital to find out how Jo was.

"But I've already saddled some of the ponies," Krista pointed out. "I thought Jo would want us to carry on as normal."

In the yard, Shandy, Kiki and Drifter were ready for action. Nathan was checking Drifter's girth and already getting on board his favourite pony.

My Magical Pony

Rob shook his head. "We can't run a trek without a grown-up to supervise it," he pointed out.

Krista frowned. Out of the corner of her eye she saw Drifter start forward and Nathan rein him back too strongly. "But *you're* here," she said to Rob.

"I'm going to the hospital. That leaves just you, Krista. I'm sorry – we'll have to cancel."

"Loosen the rein!" Krista yelled at Nathan, as Drifter reared up, plunged down and kicked out with his back legs. He was trying to get rid of the rider who was hurting his mouth.

Nathan hung on as Drifter crashed around the yard. "Whoa!" he shouted, pulling even harder.

54

Falling Leaves

"Steer him round to the left, use your right leg to turn him in a tight circle!" Krista yelled.

Nathan managed to follow her instructions and gradually Drifter stopped bucking and came to a standstill by his stable door. "What happened?" he asked as he slid shakily to the ground.

Krista stormed across the yard to join him. "You hurt his mouth, you idiot! There's no need to yank at the reins like that." She took them and stroked Drifter's sweaty neck. "There, boy, you're fine. Hush now!"

"See, that's what I mean," Rob pointed out as he too strode across. "Ponies are not predictable creatures – there's always something unexpected happening. Are you OK, Nathan?"

My Magical Pony

Nathan nodded. "I wasn't expecting him to bomb off as soon as I got in the saddle."

"He didn't bomb off!" Krista said sharply. "You know Drifter's lively and a bit edgy. You should have been ready."

"OK, cut it out," Rob told them.  "Listen, Krista, you've just seen the proof of why we need to cancel lessons and treks until Jo's better. I can't be responsible for someone getting hurt, and neither can you."

"Thanks, Nathan!" Krista muttered, blaming him though she knew it wasn't really his fault. She led Drifter into

his stable and took off his saddle.

By now, others had begun to arrive and Krista heard Rob explaining the situation to the parents who were dropping off their kids.

"I quite agree," Mrs Owen said, turning her car around in the yard and telling Holly to get back in. "There's nothing you can do except cancel the lessons and wait until Jo is better."

Alice arrived next. Quickly Krista told her what had happened.

"I'll stop and help you muck out," she decided. "At least we can make sure that the ponies are well looked after."

Krista nodded. "I promised Jo I'd take care of them."

My Magical Pony

"Good." Rob got into his Land Rover. "I'm leaving them in your capable hands. With a bit of luck, the doctors at the hospital will soon find out what's wrong with Jo and they'll be able to put it right. We should know more after I've visited."

Alice held up both hands to show him that her fingers were crossed. "Tell her to get better quick!"

"Tell her we're looking after everyone here!" Krista shouted after Rob as he drove out of the yard.

Krista and Alice worked non-stop. They wheeled barrow after barrow of soiled straw to the muck heap, they brushed floors, spread

new straw and carted heavy bales of sweet-smelling hay from the barn. Then they checked tack in the tack room, polishing bits until they were spotless and rubbing saddle soap into saddles to make the leather clean and supple.

"Phew, my arms ache!" Alice groaned, tucking her long auburn hair behind her ears. She sat on the bench outside the tack room, sleeves rolled up, tucking into a cheese sandwich which her mum had packed for her.

Krista looked at her watch. It was midday and there was still no sign of Rob, and no news from the hospital. "I'm going to take a look at Duchess and Frankie," she told Alice. "I won't be long."

My Magical Pony

She walked briskly into the lane and out to the field where the new arrivals stood waiting at the gate. Duchess whinnied noisily, obviously expecting a treat.

"Yes, you greedy thing, I've brought you an apple!" Krista smiled, retrieving a wrinkled specimen from her jacket pocket. She'd found a row of them on the window sill in the tack room – obviously left there by Jo ready to

hand out to the ponies. Krista held the apple flat on her palm and offered it to the chestnut mare.

Duchess snaffled the apple. Her big teeth crunched into it.

Falling Leaves

"And here's one for you!" Krista told little Frankie, who nudged her arm as his mother chomped away.

The foal nipped the second apple from Krista's hand as soon as it appeared from the pocket.

"Cheeky!" she laughed. Then she turned up the collar of her jacket. "Brr! It's so-o-o cold!"

A strong wind blew off the sea and up the moor side, catching the Hartfell fields with full force so that leaves fell from the trees and spiralled through the air. It raised them from the hedgerows, scattered them across the short grass and blew them in flurries across the fields.

"One white sock, send him right away ..."

Krista murmured. She felt sad as she repeated the rhyme. "Two white socks, keep him but a day."

Frankie finished his apple and nuzzled her hand for more. His bright eyes were full of fun.

"Three white socks, give him to a friend ..."

Frankie trotted a short way from the gate, kicked and bucked out of sheer joy, then trotted back again on his four white legs. His fuzzy mane and tail blew in the wind.

Falling Leaves

"… Four white socks, keep him till the end!" Krista whispered with tears in her eyes.

Then she hurried back to the yard to help Alice put hay in nets for the evening feed.

"Let's keep busy and try not to think," Alice suggested.

Krista nodded. "Good idea."

But minutes seemed like hours and hours felt like days when you were waiting for news and fearing the worst.

"Jo has to stay in hospital," Rob told Krista and Alice. He'd spent the whole day at her bedside and had at last returned to Hartfell with the news they'd been dreading.

"What's wrong with her?" Alice asked,

while Krista stood by with a sinking heart.

"They still don't know." Rob ran a hand over his eyes then dragged it over his nose and mouth in a weary gesture. "They're doing all sorts of tests and scans, but the results won't be ready for a while."

"How is she?" Suddenly Krista recalled the sound of the ambulance siren and the sight of Jo lying unconscious on the floor of the tack room. She swallowed hard and tried not to panic.

"She's conscious, but she's not saying much, poor thing. It must be awful waiting for the medics to find out what's wrong with you."

Alice pursed her lips. "Should we call her family and tell them?"

Falling Leaves

"There's no family," Rob began. "Jo's parents died. I don't think there's anyone else."

"Yes, there's a sister in America!" Krista remembered, turning to Rob. "You know – Bonnie's mum!" Bonnie had visited Jo one Easter and turned out to be an expert rider. She'd given Krista a hard time with her know-it-all attitude, but in the end the two girls had become friends.

"Oh yeah, that's right." Rob considered this for a while. "America's an awful long way away. Besides, how would we trace them?"

"Ask Jo for their phone number," Krista suggested.

So she and Alice waited while Rob called Jo's hospital number and talked to her.

They saw his face crease up into a frown and then watched as he walked away to talk in private. When he came back he had slipped the phone back into his pocket.

"No good," Rob reported. "Jo doesn't want me to call her sister."

"Why not?" Krista and Alice asked together.

"Apparently they had a row a while back. Now the sisters aren't on speaking terms."

"But Jo's sick. Surely the family need to know!" Krista objected.

Rob nodded. "That's what I said to Jo, but she won't listen. She reckons she'll be up and out of hospital by the end of the weekend, so there's no need to phone anyone."

The three stood in silence in the windy

yard. The autumn day was drawing to a close and it was time to bring in the ponies from the fields.

"I don't think Jo's right," Rob said quietly. "The way I look at it, they'll have to keep her in for at least a week, maybe more, for the test results to come through."

Alice gasped. "But what'll happen here?"

Rob shook his head. "I've no idea. I'm busy lecturing all next week, so I can't help out."

"It's half-term. *We* can!" Krista said, looking at Alice, who nodded.

But Rob sighed. "That's not realistic. Face it, Krista, we're going to have to look for an adult who can step in."

"But who?" Krista pleaded. Every grown-up she could think of had a full-time job of their own.

"And what if we can't find anyone?" Alice added.

Rob's face looked deadly serious. "Then we'll have to spend tomorrow looking for new homes for the ponies."

"But I promised Jo I'd look after them, here!" Krista cried. "It was the last thing she asked me!"

"And I'm saying it's not realistic," Rob replied.

Falling Leaves

"Listen … look, you can't! Rob, this is Drifter we're talking about, and Kiki and Misty and Comanche!" Krista could hardly get the words out, she was so upset. "You're talking about getting rid of Duchess and Frankie!"

Rob looked her in the eyes and nodded. He delivered the words Krista never thought she'd hear. "That's right. We have no choice – if we can't find someone to help out, Hartfell will have to close."

Chapter Six

"I've broken my promise!" Krista sobbed. "I've let everyone down – Jo, Apollo, Scottie, Comanche …"

Her mum gave her a big hug. "Some promises just can't be kept," she said softly. Rob had brought Krista back from the stables and explained the situation before he'd driven on.

"Especially when you make them on the spur of the moment." Krista's dad agreed. "Jo would never have asked you if she'd been thinking clearly."

Falling Leaves

"I don't care. I said I'd do it, but Rob won't let me. He says everyone has to leave – Kiki and Misty and Duchess …" Every one of the ponies' names made Krista want to cry some more. "And I promised little Frankie he could stay at Hartfell forever, and he'll never trust anyone ever again if we send him away now!"

"Nothing lasts forever," Krista's mum said sadly.

"Come and sit by the fire." Her dad invited her to cosy up next to him on the sofa. "You know, in a sudden fit of generosity when I was a kid I once promised a mate of mine called David that he could ride my bike home then keep it for good. He was dead pleased. But my mum and dad had different ideas.

My Magical Pony

My dad went right around to his house and demanded the bike back. I thought I'd never be able to look David in the face ever again."

"How old were you?" Krista sniffed.

"Five."

"That's different then." She smiled weakly. "I'm ten. And a pony isn't the same as a bike.

Falling Leaves

A pony's a living, breathing animal with thoughts and feelings."

"Yes, and I'm sure Rob will ring around tonight and tomorrow morning and find good temporary homes for Comanche and the rest," Krista's mum soothed.

To Krista this sounded better than the Hartfell ponies vanishing for good. She nodded then took a deep breath, drying her tears.

"And who knows," her dad went on, going upstairs to bring down her pyjamas and warm them by the fire, "Jo could get better more quickly than Rob expects. We could be back to normal by the end of the week."

*

Nevertheless, there was no spring in Krista's step as she said goodbye to her mum and dad and took the cliff path early next morning, and she took no notice of the magic spot as she passed.

Shining Star watched and waited from a distance. *Why does Krista not call me?* he wondered. *The trouble I foresaw has come to pass. There is a great sadness amongst the ponies. It is here. It is now.*

But Krista walked on, her head hanging, thinking miserably about the way things had turned out and of the promises she had broken.

"Good news," Rob announced as she walked on to the stable yard. "I've already

74

found new homes for six of the ponies."

"Cool," Krista nodded, without meaning what she said. "So tell me."

Rob led her round the yard from stable to stable. "Holly is taking Woody back to Mill Lane, and her dad has agreed to take in Kiki as well."

Krista stroked the bay pony's nose. "You hear that, Kiki? You're going to live at Mill House with Woody."

Rob walked on. "And Duchess and Frankie at the end there are going to Alan Lewis's place."

"Moorside Farm?" Krista checked. She knew Alan and his little son, Will. "Cool," she said again. So far so good.

My Magical Pony

"You'll like it on the Lewis farm," she promised Frankie, who had poked his head over the stable door. She felt a pang of guilt as she stroked his neck. "When is Alan coming with his trailer?"

"Later this morning. I've got a bit of a problem with Apollo and Scottie though."

Krista frowned and sighed. "Doesn't anybody want them?"

"It's not that. There's a yard over at Maythorne with space to stable them. But no spare trailer to pick them up in until later today."

"Are you going to fit in a visit to Jo?" Krista broke in. She stopped beside Comanche's door and ran her hand through

his thick brown mane.

"Yep. I'll try to get down there this afternoon. By that time I should be able to put her mind at rest over what's happening to most of her 'babies'!"

"Any news this morning?" Krista's voice was dull. In spite of what her mum and dad had said the night before, she couldn't shake the feeling that she had broken her promise and that Jo would feel totally let down.

Rob nodded. "I rang the hospital. Jo had a quiet night, but they're still not sure what the

problem is. They think it might be neurological – something to do with the messages the brain sends around the nervous system."

"That sounds bad."

"Not always. Let's keep looking on the bright side," Rob insisted. He answered his phone, which had begun to ring. "Yep … No … OK … well never mind, thanks for thinking about it." He clicked off his phone and turned back to Krista. "That was Matt Simons about Comanche. I was hoping he'd be able to keep him up at Cragside."

"But he can't?" Krista prompted.

Rob shook his head. "They're going away for a few days, so it's no good."

As if understanding that they were talking

78

about him, Comanche thrust his nose between them and gave Krista a shove. *What happens now?* he seemed to say.

Krista put her arms around the piebald's neck. "Don't worry," she whispered. "We won't leave you here by yourself."

But by the afternoon the yard was emptying and poor Comanche still had no home.

Krista had said goodbye to Scottie and Apollo, who had been driven off at last in the Maythorne yard's plush white horse-box, their long, slim legs booted and their flowing tails bandaged for travel. She'd waved Woody and Kiki out of the yard, towed in a smaller box by Holly's mum.

My Magical Pony

The two ponies had whinnied loudly as they were driven down the lane. More trailers had arrived for other ponies.

This is awful! Krista thought each time, feeling that her heart was being twisted and wrung out as the stables gradually emptied. And somehow it got worse as the day went on.

"Are Duchess and Frankie ready to go?" Rob asked. He'd spotted Alan's Land Rover and trailer in the lane.

Krista led the mare out first. Duchess didn't like the look of the trailer, so they had to coax her up the ramp. She stamped and braced her front legs, pulling on the lead rope and refusing to enter until Alan offered her a handful of hay from inside the box.

Falling Leaves

"Come on, girl!" Krista coaxed. If the mother wouldn't come, they had no chance of getting the foal in.

Duchess flared her nostrils and stretched her neck for the hay. At last they managed to edge her forward.

"This one doesn't want to leave!" Alan grinned. "And who can blame her? Jo keeps these animals in the lap of luxury!"

"Good girl!" Krista murmured as Duchess came up the ramp. She tied her securely and watched Frankie hurry up after her.

Rob lifted the ramp and bolted it in place. The last Krista saw of Frankie was with his head turned towards her, his ears laid flat and a look of fear in his eyes.

81

My Magical Pony

"That's it for now," Rob told Krista, who waved Alan out of the yard. "Can you hang on here while I slip down to see Jo?"

She nodded. "Did you find anyone for Comanche yet?" she asked, spotting the lonely piebald peering over his table door.

Rob shook his head. "To be honest, he's the one I'm struggling with. At this rate, he'll be the only one left."

Which is another promise I'm breaking, Krista thought, plodding heavily across the yard to comfort Comanche. *I don't seem to be able to*

open my mouth without letting someone down!

Poor Comanche nuzzled her as if to say,
What's going on? Why is everyone leaving?

"See you soon!" Rob called as he drove off.

Krista looked round the yard and sighed
at the sight of the empty stables. Now that
she was alone, she began to question Rob's
big decision to get rid of all the ponies.
"Why can't we ring Jo's sister in America,
like Alice said?"

Comanche snorted and stamped his heavy
feet. It was as if he was saying, "Yes, why
can't we?"

And it was so sad to see the empty stables
and to think of all the ponies arriving at their
new homes, looking round bewildered,

whinnying for their friends. No, Krista decided she couldn't stand it.

Leaving Comanche and running towards Jo's house, Krista went inside. She dashed into the kitchen where Jo kept her list of important phone numbers on the notice board. Farradays Feed Supplies, John Carter the vet, Sean Johnson the farrier ... down the list until she came to Jo's friends ... Rob, Chris and Ruth ... someone called Jackie with a long number after her name.

"This could be it!" Krista decided, her heart in her mouth. The code could definitely be American. But dare Krista ring the number? She stood in the kitchen, trying to decide what to do.

84

Falling Leaves

Then Krista heard a long, lonely whinny from Comanche and this made up her mind. "Do it!" she said out loud, carefully dialling Jackie's number. "Jo's sister needs to know what's going on. Whatever they've been arguing about, this is an emergency and families are meant to stick together!"

Krista listened to the strange dialling tone. For a long time no one answered. Then there was a click and a voice spoke. "Hi there, this is Jackie Scott speaking."

Krista gasped. This was it! "Hello, I'm ringing from England. Is that Jo Weston's sister?"

"Who is this?" the woman's voice said. She sounded surprised.

85

"My name's Krista. I help Jo out on the stable yard."

Surprise turned quickly to suspicion. "What do you want?"

"Jo's sick. She's been taken into hospital. Am I speaking to her sister?"

"Yes. But I don't know why you're calling me. I haven't spoken to Jo for six months."

In the background, Krista heard another voice. "Mom, what's going on? Who are you talking to?"

Krista felt certain this was Bonnie. "Maybe I could speak to your daughter," she suggested. "Bonnie and I are friends. I met her when she came to stay here."

"… Mom, give me a break, tell me who you're talking to."

"Bonnie, quit that. This is not your business." There was a pause, then Jackie Scott came back on the phone to Krista. "Listen, whoever you are, there's no way I want to get dragged in to my sister's affairs."

"But she's in hospital," Krista protested. "She needs help."

"And I'm not the one to give it," came the swift reply. "That's all I have to say."

To Krista's dismay, the phone went dead.

87

She stood a while, lost in thought, then she went out into the yard.

The wind was blowing stronger than ever. It rattled at the iron rings driven into the stone walls, it whipped in and out of the empty stables, driving fallen leaves into dark corners.

"Hopeless!" Krista said in a small, lost voice. Jo's sister was not prepared to listen. Krista had tried and failed.

Comanche stared forlornly across the empty yard. The wind blew and the autumn leaves fell.

Chapter Seven

"Krista!" Shining Star called her name.

He looked down from a great distance and saw her standing sadly in the stable yard. *Why doesn't she come to the magic spot?* he wondered.

Krista looked up at the dreary autumn sky. Her heart felt heavy, she was sadder than she had ever been before. *What can I do?* she thought.

Sighing and shaking her head, Krista walked across the yard to prepare a bucket of feed for Comanche. She scooped the oat and bran mix from the bin, breathing in

the sweet smell of molasses. "Poor Comanche," she said out loud, "he must feel like nobody wants him!"

The little piebald smelt his food and whinnied.

"Here," Krista murmured, carrying the bucket across. She watched him lower his head to feed, remembering Jackie Scott's harsh tone on the phone, even when Bonnie had tried to intervene. "I bet Bonnie would want to help if she knew what was happening!" Krista muttered quietly. "Bonnie's a good rider and she loves horses …"

Suddenly Krista stopped mumbling and cocked her head to one side. *Yeah, Bonnie would help. But she doesn't know what's going on.*

Falling Leaves

*So how do I get through to her without her mum
standing in the way ...?*

"I know!" The cry broke from Krista,
making Comanche raise his head. *What now?*

"Wait here!" Krista told a puzzled
Comanche. "Don't worry about being on your
own. Rob will be back soon. Anyway, I'll try
not to be too long!"

"Shining Star, I've been so stupid!" Krista
stood on the magic spot, calling for her
magical pony. "I was so sad about the ponies
leaving Hartfell that I never even thought to
come and find you!"

Waiting for what seemed like an age,
Krista stared up at the clouds.

91

My Magical Pony

They swept overhead, driven off the sea by the strong wind, skimming the rocky moor top and sailing on inland.

"At last!" Shining Star said to himself from his home in Galishe. He spread his white wings and rose above the fields of sparkling white flowers and streams that glittered like a million diamonds. He flew so fast that the land below began to tilt and vanish. Then the magical pony entered a tunnel of whirling light and dark, speeding between stars and planets until he came to Earth.

"Shining Star, you came!" Running up the hill from the magic spot, Krista flung her arms around her magical pony. She basked in his glittering light.

Falling Leaves

"I was waiting for you to call," he told her softly. "What is the matter? What has happened?"

"The ponies at Hartfell have been sent away!" she gasped. "All except Comanche, and he's been left there all alone. It's awful – the yard is deserted except for him!"

"And how has this come about?" Shining Star's voice was always low and unhurried. It helped to calm Krista so that she could explain.

She told Star about Jo's illness and her own promise to take care of the ponies, and how she'd broken it because Rob had sent them all away except Comanche, and then she'd phoned Jo's sister in Colorado and

Falling Leaves

Jackie Scott had refused point-blank to help.

The magical pony listened attentively. "Then we must fly to visit the sister," he decided in an instant. "Come, Krista, climb on my back. There is no time to lose."

Shining Star's magic was so strong that he could fly across continents in the blink of an eye, passing through day and night, soaring over high mountains and crossing vast seas.

Above the world, Krista looked down on the glittering blue ocean. Star's wings beat strongly, his silken white mane streamed back from his face. She held her breath and gazed down as they passed through white clouds and were buffeted by winds. On the sea,

tiny ships ploughed straight white lines.
A small island broke the smooth surface,
fringed by white sand. Then the ocean was
empty again as they flew on and on until they
came to land with wide rivers and open
plains, leading on to forest and hills, blue
lakes, then bare mountains rising towards
Krista and Shining Star.

"America!" Krista breathed, leaning low
over Star's neck. The wind took her breath
away, she was filled with a sense of wonder.

"It is an immense, beautiful land," Star said.
His wings had not missed a beat during the
long voyage and now they were nearing its
end. He looked down on the snow-topped
mountains dotted with lakes. "We have

96

Falling Leaves

arrived soon after dawn on the day which has just ended in England," he explained to Krista. "You have not yet made the phone call to Jackie Scott."

"And do Bonnie and her parents live here?" Krista asked, amazed by the mountains and by the rolling green slopes between.

My Magical Pony

As Star flew closer to the ground, she made out black and white dots scattered in the valleys – cows grazing – and then a ranch house at the end of a long, winding track, and horses in a corral, and finally two figures wearing cowboy hats walking out of a barn.

"This is the home of the Scott family. Ben Scott has lived here since he was born. His fathers have farmed this land for more than a hundred years."

"It's so cool!" Krista sighed as they swept low over the ranch. The house was built of wood, with a long porch overlooking a corral where several horses were tethered. The man and woman who had walked out of the barn untied two of the horses and rode out towards

the nearest meadow where cows were grazing.

"We need to bring the cattle in by the end of next week," the man was saying. "The forecast is for snow."

Krista didn't hear the woman's reply because Shining Star had flown quickly on. "Was that Bonnie's mum and dad?" she asked.

"Ben and Jackie Scott. Your friend, Bonnie, is up early this morning. She's riding a trail west of here, looking for a lost cow and calf."

Though Krista trusted her magical pony to fly low over the ground and find Bonnie, she had no idea of what to say when they found her. "How do I explain how come we're here without giving away your secret?" she wanted to know.

My Magical Pony

Star swooped down between tall pine trees, skimming the ground with his broad wings. He saw a black and white cow with her calf tucked away down a narrow draw, well out of sight of the main trail. "Talk to Bonnie, show her these lost creatures. Do not mention my magic."

"But she'll think it's crazy – me dropping out of the sky from nowhere!" For the first time since she and Shining Star had come up with the plan, Krista hit a big snag. "Bonnie nearly found out about you before, when she visited Hartfell, remember! Maybe we shouldn't risk it after all."

"Trust me," was all her magical pony said as he landed gently.

Falling Leaves

So Krista slipped from his back and waited
on the trail for Bonnie to arrive.

Chapter Eight

"Krista?" Bonnie looked down from the saddle at the lonely figure on the trail. Her jaw dropped and her mouth fell open in sheer surprise. "Is this really you, or am I dreaming?"

"Hi, Bonnie," Krista said, walking slowly towards her.

"Jeez, why didn't you say you were coming to visit? How did you get here? Are you alone? Who drove you from the airport?"

"Hey, give me a chance!" Krista tried to grin and duck the questions. "Aren't you pleased to see me?"

Falling Leaves

Bonnie swung down from the heavy saddle and led her chestnut quarter horse towards Krista. "Sure I'm glad, but I'm totally shocked too. You're the last person I was expecting to see!"

Krista looked up at the wide canopy of branches. She glanced at the steep slopes of pink granite and at the thorn and sage bushes growing in the crevices. "Are you looking for a cow and calf?" she asked.

"Sure thing. Did you see them?"

Krista nodded and led her friend back to the narrow draw. "They're hiding in the bushes down there," she explained.

"Hey, good job!" Nimbly nipping back up into the saddle, Bonnie urged her horse

down the gully, forced the cows out from behind the willows and herded them back up towards Krista. "Don't let them get past you!" she yelled.

"What do I do to stop them?"

"Stand there with your arms and legs wide apart. Say, yip, cow!"

Falling Leaves

"Yip, cow!" Krista blocked the way as best she could.

The mother cow lowered her head and snorted, but she soon turned around with her calf to face Bonnie and her horse.

At that moment, Bonnie unhooked a long rope from her saddle-horn and flung her lasso over the cow's head. Then she slid from the saddle, drawing in the rope and snaking it around a sturdy tree trunk nearby. She tied it hard and fast. "Now you're not going anywhere!" she told the cow.

"Neat!" Krista said. "I'm impressed – you're a real cowgirl!"

Bonnie tutted and tilted the broad brim of her stetson back from her forehead.

"OK, so I have a zillion questions, apart from the obvious!" she exclaimed. "How are you doing? Are you still riding the Hartfell ponies? How's Kiki? Is Jo still winning three-day events with Apollo?"

"I'm good," Krista replied, going up to Bonnie's horse and stroking him. "Except for one big problem, and it's to do with your aunt and the ponies."

Keeping one wary eye on the tethered cow, Bonnie frowned. "I don't get to hear much about Aunt Jo any more. My mom had a big bust up with her."

"Yeah, how come?" Luckily for Krista, Bonnie had led straight into the subject she wanted to talk about. "What happened there?"

Falling Leaves

"You don't want to know!" Bonnie sighed. She watched the calf go up to the mother and pull at her udder for milk. "It was my dad's fault, I guess. Mom was all set to visit last spring, but then he has a change of heart and says she can't go to England because there's too much work to do here on the ranch – it was the cattle round-up the same week. And that was the start of it."

"Your mum cancelled her trip?"

"Yes. And Jo thought Mom was crazy to follow my dad's orders and so then they had World War Three over it. They haven't spoken since."

"That's stupid," Krista muttered.

"Yeah, but you know what families are like.

And my dad can be pretty strict, which Jo
doesn't see. Honestly though, I was on Jo's side
– I think Mom should've stood up to him."

"It would be good if the two sisters could
be friends again," Krista pointed out. She
was ready now to tell Bonnie about the big
problem at Hartfell. "Especially since Jo is
sick," she added.

Bonnie stared at her. "Sick?" she echoed.

"Yeah, she's in hospital. They don't know
what's wrong."

"So what about the ponies?" Bonnie's
mind flew straight to the main issue. "Who's
looking after them?"

Krista took a deep breath, searching
between the tall trees for a glimpse of

Shining Star. But the magical pony stayed well hidden. "Me. I'm doing it."

"Alone?"

Krista nodded. "But now they think I can't manage, so they've started trailering the ponies out to new homes. There's only Comanche left at Hartfell."

My Magical Pony

"Oh my goodness, poor old Comanche!" The news struck Bonnie hard. She put her hands over her eyes and rubbed her temples. "That's awful! And the others might hate their new homes. They could pine and fall sick!"

"So that's why I'm here," Krista went on quietly. "Bonnie, you have to persuade your mum to fly over to England and help."

Bonnie frowned. "I don't know – it's more my dad's fault, remember. We're just coming up to fall round-up. I don't think he'll let her go."

In the distance, Krista saw a faint glow in the shadow of the trees. She knew that Shining Star was drawing closer. "Talk to him," Krista pleaded. "Tell him that Jo hasn't got anyone else she can rely on!"

110

Falling Leaves

Bonnie nodded. "I'll give it a go," she agreed, without seeing the magical pony emerge from the trees. "But I don't know if it'll do any good. Hey, Jethro, what's up, boy?"

The quarter horse had spotted Shining Star and raised his head to give a shrill whinny of greeting. Then he stamped his hoof and pawed the ground.

"Oh my!" Bonnie gasped, spinning around to see the beautiful white winged pony surrounded by a silver glow.

Star approached steadily, trailing a shining mist through the shadowy forest.

"Do not be afraid," he told Bonnie.

What is he doing? Krista wondered. For the first time ever, Shining Star had revealed

his secret to another person.

"What *is* this?" Bonnie demanded, striking her forehead in a gesture of astonishment. "Now I really am dreaming!"

Her chestnut horse and the cow and calf fell quiet as Star came near.

"Listen to what Krista says," he told Bonnie.

Falling Leaves

"There is much trouble at Hartfell. Only your mother can help."

Wide-eyed, Bonnie nodded slowly. She felt the magical pony's silver dust surround her and suddenly she felt totally calm and certain of what she had to do. "I'll work on my dad," she promised. "I'm his little girl. He listens to me."

"Good," Shining Star told her, breathing over her and sheltering her beneath his wings. "Your heart is true. You will not disappoint us."

Then with a toss of his head he told Krista to climb on to his back. He spread his wings and beat them gently, sending a silver shower of dust over Bonnie and her horse, Jethro, before rising through the trees.

Krista held tight. Below them, she could see Bonnie staring into the sky, shading her eyes with one hand.

"Now she knows your secret," Krista murmured. She felt scared of what might follow.

"Ah!" Star replied, rising higher. He flew over the Scotts' ranch, over the pink mountains towards the great plains.

"What do you mean, 'Ah!'?"

Star flew on for a while without speaking. He gathered speed and the world below tilted and became a tunnel of silver light into which they flew.

"I mean that Bonnie will not remember our meeting," he explained.

114

Falling Leaves

Lights whirled about Krista's head. A great wind roared through the tunnel, and with it a storm of glittering dust.

"I breathed my magic dust over her head," Shining Star went on. "Bonnie will forget our visit, but she will remember what you have told her. When she looks back upon this morning's meeting, it will seem to her to have been a dream."

Chapter Nine

The magic journey soon came to an end and
Shining Star landed in the yard at Hartfell.
Comanche stood in his stable, neighing
loudly at the sight of the white winged pony
with Krista on his back.

"Hush, Comanche, it's OK!" Krista soothed
as she slid to the ground. She felt a chill in
the air as the sun disappeared behind the
buildings and left the stable yard in shadow.
She turned to Shining Star. "Am I back in
Sunday evening?"

Star nodded. "It is exactly the moment

before you went into the house to make
your phone call," he told her. "Rob is at the
hospital. At this moment the ponies are
arriving at their new stables."

"And how are they?" she asked, knowing
that Shining Star could see these things.

"Holly is trying to make Kiki eat from a
hay-net," Star replied, his eyes looking far
into the distance, his ears pricked as if he
could hear. "The pony will not eat. She stands
with her head hanging low."

"And what about little Frankie? How is he
getting on at Alan Lewis's place?"

"He looks lost," Star told her. "He stands in
a dark corner and trembles, even though his
mother is there."

My Magical Pony

"Oh, poor Frankie!" Krista's worst fears seemed to be coming true. "I knew they wouldn't settle in their new places. And I'm sure it's the same for the others too."

"So you must make your phone call to America," Star urged. "And perhaps this time the answer will be different."

For the second time Krista screwed up her courage to ring Jackie Scott. Again came the strange dialling tone and the long delay.

Falling Leaves

"Hi there, this is Jackie Scott speaking," a voice said.

"Hello, I'm ringing from England. Is that Jo Weston's sister?"

"Who is this?" Jackie Scott asked, sounding surprised.

"My name's Krista. I help Jo out at the stable yard."

"What do you want?" Jackie asked suspiciously.

"Jo's sick," Krista said, recalling her magical meeting with Bonnie on the mountain trail. She hoped with all her might that Bonnie had kept her promise and talked to her dad.

"I'm sorry to hear that," Jackie said in a low voice. "But you should know, I haven't spoken to my sister in six months."

In the background another voice broke in. "Mom, what's going on? Who's on the phone?"

"It's your friend, Krista, from England. She's telling me about your Aunt Jo."

"Here, give me the phone," Bonnie said, and this time her mum didn't resist or tell her that it wasn't her business. "Hi, Krista!" Bonnie said.

This is better! Krista thought, her hopes rising a little. "Hi, Bonnie. Did you talk to your dad? Does he know Jo's in hospital?"

"Yeah, I got this weird message earlier today – like a dream, only not a dream. I sort of knew something bad had happened, so I called the hospital in Whitton and found

120

out all I could. Then I talked to Dad."

"Bonnie, give me the phone back."
Alarmed by what she heard, Jackie Scott tried
to butt in.

"Wait, Mom! Krista, this is what I found
out – the doctors are talking about a possible
tumour on Jo's brain …"

Krista gasped and grasped the receiver a
little harder. This sounded really, really bad.

Then Jackie succeeded in taking back the
phone. "Oh God, is this true?" she asked.

Krista shook her head. "I didn't know that.
But I was the one who found Jo unconscious,
and she's been having bad headaches. The
hospital is doing tests …"

"Mom, you need to go and visit!"

My Magical Pony

Bonnie's voice came through loud and clear. "This is your sister we're talking about. Whatever Dad says, you need to go!"

Helpless, Krista listened to the far-off conversation. As Bonnie urged her mom to leave the ranch and come to England, a third voice suddenly cut in.

"OK, will someone tell me what's going on around here!" the man demanded.

"Dad, Mom's heard the bad news about Jo," Bonnie said. "I told you she'd soon find out and that it was serious!"

"That still doesn't mean she's ditching stuff here and jetting off halfway across the world," Ben Scott insisted. "It's round-up week, remember!"

Falling Leaves

"You have to let her go!" Bonnie yelled. "You can't lay down the law like this!"

"Want to bet?" Bonnie's dad argued. Then the voices went fuzzy, as if Jackie had put her hand over the mouthpiece.

"Try to come, Mrs Scott," Krista pleaded. "We need you!"

There was another long pause then Jackie Scott spoke again. "Leave it with me," she told Krista. "I'll call you back, OK!"

For half an hour Krista paced the floor in the kitchen at Hartfell. She took a can of Coke from the fridge and drank it, studying the photos of Jo on Apollo which were pinned to the notice board. Jo was smiling at the camera,

dressed in show-jumping gear, looking proud
and happy.

"Please get better!" Krista murmured.

Jo's cats came and rubbed themselves
against Krista's legs. They too were missing Jo.

When the phone rang, Krista ran to pick
it up. But instead of Jackie Scott, she heard
Rob's voice.

Falling Leaves

"Hi Krista, Rob here. Listen, I'm still at the hospital. I hoped you'd be hanging on there."

"Yes, I couldn't leave Comanche all alone. I can stay as long as you need me."

"OK, good. But call home and tell your mum and dad where you are. I could be a while yet."

Krista could tell that Rob was worried. "What's happened?" she asked. "Have the doctors found out what's wrong with Jo?"

"They did a brain scan and they think there's a lump – tumour inside the skull, pressing on to a part of the brain," he replied quietly. "… Krista, did you hear that?"

Swallowing hard, Krista said yes. She tried to sound surprised. "That's serious, isn't it?"

125

"Yes. But they're hoping it's nothing too nasty and that they can operate and take the tumour away."

"OK, good."

"Krista, can you ask your mum to come over and stay with you at Hartfell tonight? I need to stay here with Jo."

"Yeah, sure."

"Good. Are you sure you're OK?"

"Yes, fine. I'll take care of Comanche."

"Good girl. I'll call you first thing tomorrow. Bye."

"Bye." Krista heard the phone click and go dead. Leaving the back door open, she ran into the yard to tell Shining Star the latest news.

The magical pony stood in the empty yard.

Falling Leaves

His silver glow brightened the shadows and gave Krista hope. "You are doing well," he told her. "Now we must wait."

"Will you stay here tonight?" she pleaded. "Then Comanche won't be alone."

From his stable the little piebald stretched his head forward and snickered.

"I will wait with you," Star replied, bending his beautiful head to let Krista stroke it.

Then the phone rang again, making Krista jump. She shot back into the house. "Hello, Hartfell Stables, Krista here!" she gabbled.

"This is Ben Scott speaking – Jackie's husband."

"Yes!" Krista cut in eagerly. She held her breath, unable to tell what Mr Scott would say next. He sounded stern, like a head teacher or a policeman.

"Are you the young lady who spoke to my wife and daughter a while back?"

"Yes!" Krista gasped. *He's going to say no!* she thought. *All this planning – me calling for Shining Star and flying out to the ranch – has been for nothing!*

Falling Leaves

"Well, you did a good job on my little girl," Ben Scott went on. "And she did a good job on me. I got all the tears and the 'Please let Mommy go!' routine."

Krista held the phone to her ear, feeling her heart sink. Ben Scott was a strict, hard man. He was going to tell her no!

"In the end I said OK, go, get on the plane. I can hire an extra hand for round-up – what the heck!"

"'Go'?" Krista echoed, feeling her legs go weak and her hand shake.

"Yep," Ben Scott confirmed. "I called to let you know that Jackie's packing her bags. In two hours' time, she'll be on the plane to England!"

Chapter Ten

There was frost in the air when Krista woke up next morning. The fallen leaves in the stable yard were crisp underfoot.

"I'll make breakfast while you go out and feed Comanche," Krista's mum told her. She'd spent the night at Jo's house with Krista. They were still waiting for more news from the hospital.

Zipping up her jacket, Krista strode outside. *At least I needn't worry about Comanche, with Shining Star to keep him company,* she thought.

Falling Leaves

Sure enough, the piebald pony stood with his head over the partition wall, happily watching Star's every move and occasionally nuzzling him when he came close.

"So cool!" Krista cooed, hardly able to believe that her magical pony had spent the night in the stable next to Comanche's. He lit the whole place up with his shimmering silvery-white coat.

Star waited to one side as Krista came into his stable. "The news from America is good?" he checked.

Krista nodded, looking over her shoulder as she heard sounds from the lane. "Jackie Scott is on her way. Uh-oh, and so are some other people!"

My Magical Pony

As she spoke, Janey and Alice cycled
into the yard. They quickly spotted Krista
standing by the stable door.

"Hey, we couldn't stay away!" Alice cried.
"Even though the ponies are gone, we came
to see if we could help!"

"Quick, hide!" Krista whispered to Star.
Janey and Alice mustn't discover him here.

But he stood calmly, and even moved to
the door to study the new arrivals.

"Hey, who's this cute little thing?" Janey
cried, running over. "Isn't he the moorland
pony who sometimes hangs around?"

Taking a deep breath, Krista nodded.
Of course – Shining Star was the master of
disguise! He'd used his magic to appear as an

ordinary shaggy moorland pony who lived wild on the hills. "He's keeping Comanche company," she explained.

"Ah, sweet!" Janey and Alice made a fuss of the newcomer, while yet another familiar face appeared in the yard.

"Hey, Nathan!" Krista called.

Nathan sauntered up. "I thought I could clean some tack, or maybe check the fields and clear off any ragwort and other weeds."

"Good idea," Krista agreed, grinning at Shining Star and going to the tack-room to hand out plastic sacks to Janey, Alice and Nathan.

She followed them out to the nearest field, gazing across the empty hillside at the slopes where Apollo, Scottie, Drifter, Shandy, Misty

and the rest should be. She frowned and shook her head. The Hartfell ponies should be here together – not split up in strange homes where they couldn't settle.

As Alice, Janey and Nathan climbed the nearest gate and began to scour the field for weeds, Krista walked back up the lane. *How long will little Frankie have to stay away?* she wondered.

"Krista!" a familiar voice yelled.

A car drove up the lane behind her. Krista turned to stare at the figure hanging out of the passenger window.

"Krista, it's me, Bonnie!"

"Oh wow! What? How?"

"I came too!" Bonnie exclaimed, her long

134

Falling Leaves

fair hair blowing in the wind. "Dad let me get on the plane. Mom, we're here, stop! Let me out of the car!"

Flinging open the door, Bonnie leaped out and hugged Krista. "How cool is this! I mean, not cool 'cos Jo is sick, but cool to be here.

My Magical Pony

Wow, you're freezing cold! Hey, smile, make like you're pleased to see me! Mom, this is Krista! Krista, meet my mom!"

Bonnie Scott was a whirlwind. Her mum was much quieter. She looked like her sister, Jo.

"Mom, you go in the house with Krista's mom and make some calls!" Bonnie suggested, five minutes after they'd arrived. "Tell all the folks who are looking after Aunty Jo's ponies to bring them back to Hartfell. Say they can trailer them back now, right this minute!"

At last Krista managed to get a word in as she and Bonnie crossed the yard to look in on Comanche. "How long can you stay?"

Falling Leaves

"For as long as it takes. Until Jo's better. Mom spoke to the hospital. They're going to do the surgery today – in fact, as we speak."

"And will she be OK?" Krista asked.

"Yeah, good. They say the surgery should do the trick – fingers crossed." Leading the way as ever, Bonnie looked in on Comanche. "Hey, old boy, remember me?"

Comanche nuzzled her hand then went straight for her pockets.

"No treats in there!" Bonnie laughed. She glanced in at Star. "Hey, are you the little guy who lives up on the moor?"

Obligingly Star shuffled up to the partition to be stroked.

"Yeah, I met you before," Bonnie recalled.
"I remember, Krista tamed you and you let her
ride bareback!"

Yeah, right! Krista thought, giving Shining
Star a secret grin.

"So come on, let's get this show on the
road!" Bonnie cried, rolling up her sleeves
ready to spread fresh straw in the stables.
"Krista, grab a wheelbarrow. Remind me
where you keep your bales!"

The whirlwind sprang into action. Straw
flew everywhere, tossed by Bonnie and
Krista over each stable door and whipped
by the wind into the far corners of the yard.
Then Nathan, Janey and Alice came back
from the field to help stuff fresh hay into

nets, ready for the return of the ponies.

"Holly's bringing Woody and Kiki back at eleven," Krista's mum reported. She and Jackie Scott had brought hot drinks out to the tack-room.

"And I'm going down to visit Jo this afternoon, when she comes out of surgery," Jackie told them.

"It'll give her such a boost to know you're over here taking care of things," Krista's mum said. "It's bound to help her get better more quickly."

The kids were back into action almost before their drinks had time to cool – checking head collars, sweeping the yard, preparing for the ponies' return.

Then Holly showed up as planned, leading
Kiki then Woody out of the trailer, straight
into their old stables.

Cheeky Woody snuck a mouthful of hay
from Comanche's net. High-stepping Kiki did
a little dance on the end of her lead-rope,
glad to be home.

Falling Leaves

Next came Scottie and Apollo in their posh Maythorne trailer, and soon the yard was buzzing with vehicles and ponies, the empty stables filling up before Krista's eyes.

"Hey Krista, we need to move the wild pony out of that end stable!" Bonnie called as Duchess and Frankie arrived. Her voice carried way above the sounds of car engines and horses' hooves. "There's no room for the mare and foal if he stays!"

Krista saw Duchess step warily down Alan Lewis's ramp into the yard. Little Frankie followed, his eyes wide, his skinny legs trembling. *Four white socks – keep him till the end!*

There were tears in Krista's eyes as she unbolted the door to the end stable and

Shining Star stepped out into the busy yard.

"This is all thanks to you," she told him quietly.

They walked together, between the cars and trailers, crossing paths with Duchess and Frankie, who skittered sideways and accidentally bumped into Star. The magical pony nudged the foal gently back towards his mother.

"Here Krista, take this head collar for your wild pony!" Bonnie cried from a distance.

"I don't need one, thanks," Krista replied, walking with Shining Star into the lane, and from there into the nearest field. "I'll tell you something," she sighed, one hand resting on Star's smooth white neck. "I never thought I'd

142

be so glad to hear Bonnie yelling orders again!"

Shining Star tossed his silky mane back from his face. "Her heart is good," he said.

"You bet!" Krista agreed. Slowly she took her hand away from Shining Star's neck. "That was a fantastic, magical journey," she murmured. "One of the best!"

"And you are happy?" he asked, looking steadily into her eyes.

She nodded. "Jo will get better. The ponies are safe. And when Jo comes home, her babies will be here to greet her!"

"Then goodbye, Krista," Shining Star said, spreading his wings, scattering his silver mist and soaring above the bare trees high into the autumn sky.

My Magical Pony

"Goodbye!" Krista murmured, rushing back to lead Frankie into his stable and to tell him not to worry – he was home for good!